EEK & ACK

THE BIG MISTAKE

written by
BLAKE A. HOENA

illustrations by
STEVE HARPSTER

Raintree is an imprint of Capstone Global Library Limited,
a company incorporated in England and Wales having its
registered office at 7 Pilgrim Street, London, EC4V 6LB –
Registered company number: 6695582

www.raintreepublishers.co.uk
myorders@raintreepublishers.co.uk

ISBN 978 1 406 27566 7
17 16 15 14 13
10 9 8 7 6 5 4 3 2 1

British Library Cataloguing in Publication Data
A full catalogue record for this book is available from the
British Library.

Printed in China by Nordica.
1013/CA21301916

TABLE OF CONTENTS

Chapter 1

BLECK'S DARE

One day Eek and Ack were
scanning the galaxy. They hoped to
find a new planet to conquer.

"Is that one?" Ack asked.

"No, silly," Eek replied. "That's just
a flying saucer."

Suddenly, their big sister Bleck stormed in. "Dad! Mum!" she yelled. "Eek and Ack are playing in the laser room!"

Bleck flashed her brothers an evil smile. "Ha! You're in trouble," she said.

"We haven't done anything yet,"
Ack said.

"But we're going to," Eek said.

"We're going to conquer a planet."

"In what?" Bleck asked. "That junky spaceship of yours?"

"Once, we flew our junky spaceship all the way to Earth," Ack bragged.

"Ha!" Bleck said. "Earthlings still use toilets that flush. Why would you want to go there?"

"Yeah, our vacuum toilets are so much better," Ack said. "And they have more buttons."

"Well, I bet you can't even conquer Earth," Bleck said.

Chapter 2

EEK HAS AN IDEA

"Forget about Bleck," said Ack.
"Let's go swimming."

"Okay," said Eek. But he was still
mad. "First we need to show Bleck
we can do anything we want."

"But how can we conquer Earth?" Ack asked. "We don't even have a BB-Blaster. Let's just go straight to the pool."

Eek ignored him. "Hmm," he thought, staring at his parents' space dome.

Eek looked up at the front window.

"I have an idea!" he shouted.

"Oh, no," Ack said. "I get worried whenever you have one of those. Things never seem to go well."

"Remember when we zapped
snottle bugs?" Eek asked his brother.

"Yeah, with my magnifying glass,"
Ack said. "They sizzled and oozed.
And they didn't smell very nice."

"Well, what if we had a giant magnifying glass?" Eek asked.

"Ooh, we could use it to zap earthlings!" Ack shouted.

"Hey," Ack said as he looked up. "Our front window looks a bit like a magnifying glass."

"Exactly!" Eek said with a very evil laugh.

The brothers removed the window.

Chapter 3

THAT'S NOT EARTH!

Eek and Ack attached the window to the spaceship. Then they blasted off into space.

The brothers zoomed across the galaxy and travelled towards Earth.

When they arrived, Eek parked their spaceship in front of the sun. Earth floated in front of them like a big blue and green marble.

Ack carefully climbed out of the spaceship.

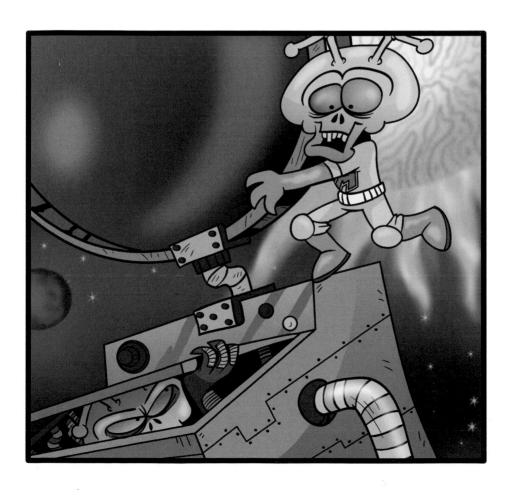

"You aim the magnifying glass," Eek told Ack.

"Please can you tell me which one is Earth again?" Ack asked.

"It's the planet on your left," Eek said.

"Um . . . okay," Ack said. "I wonder if earthlings stink as much as snottle bugs when they get zapped."

Zap!

"No, Ack! That's not Earth," Eek shouted. "I said your left!"

"Which one's my left?" Ack asked.

"On your *left* was Earth," Eek said.

"The frozen planet on your *right*, was Pluto."

"Oops . . ." Ack said.

"And it looks like you melted it,"
Eek said. "We better get out of here
before someone sees what we did."

Eek and Ack quickly zipped back
across the galaxy.

As the boys returned home, Eek said, "Now don't tell Bleck about our big mistake."

"I won't," Ack said. He wiped his head. "Flying near Earth's sun made me really hot."

"Let's go jump in the pool to cool down," Eek said.

Bleck was sitting by the pool. She was eating a treat.

"What's she eating?" Ack asked.

"I don't know," Eek said. "But it looks tasty."

"It's a Pluto-sicle," Bleck said. "They say it came from Pluto."

"Oh, no!" Eek said. "Somebody must have found out about our mistake."

"I don't care," Ack said. "I want a Pluto-sicle, too."

Eek and Ack raced each other to the Pluto-sicle stand.

At the stand, the owner was telling a story. "There it was," he said. "This ball of melted ice near Earth. I took it to make my Pluto-sicles. Aren't they tasty?"

"They certainly are!" Ack said.

"I'm not sure if this is the biggest mistake we've made," Eek said to Ack. "But it has to be the tastiest."

ABOUT THE AUTHOR

Blake Hoena has written more than 20 books for children. He once spent a whole weekend just watching his favourite science-fiction films. Those films made him wonder if he could invent some aliens who had death rays, hyperdrives, and clever equipment, but still couldn't conquer Earth. That's when he created the two young aliens Eek and Ack, who play at conquering Earth just like earthling children play at beating villains.

ABOUT THE ARTIST

Steve Harpster has loved to draw funny cartoons, mean monsters, and goofy gadgets ever since he first starting using a pencil. At school, he preferred drawing pictures for stories rather than writing them. Steve now draws funny pictures for books as his job, and that's really what he's best at. Steve lives in Ohio in America and has a sheepdog called Doodle.

GLOSSARY

conquer to defeat and take control of an enemy; Eek always wants to conquer planet Earth.

earthlings creatures from the planet Earth

galaxy a large group of stars and planets

oozed flowed out slowly

Pluto-sicle an ice lolly treat made out of ice from the planet Pluto

sizzled made a hissing noise

snottle bugs slime-filled insects that can be found on planet Gloop

tastiest best tasting

vacuum a machine that sucks up dirt or liquid

TALK ABOUT THE STORY

1. Why do you think Eek and Ack would like to conquer a planet?

2. Eek and Ack do not get along with their sister, Bleck. Do you ever fight with your siblings?

3. Imagine that Eek and Ack's parents caught them removing the window from the house. What do you think would happen?

WRITING TIME

1. In this story, Eek and Ack worked together to try to reach a goal. Write about a time when you worked with someone.

2. Create an advertisement for Pluto-sicles. Make sure you tell your customers why Pluto-sicles are so wonderful.

3. Write about your favourite character in this book. Why are they your favourite?

EXPLORING THE UNIVERSE

with Eek & Ack

Pluto was once considered the ninth planet in the Milky Way solar system. But in 2006, astronomers reclassified it as a dwarf planet. This is because it shares an orbit with other large objects, such as asteroids. True planets don't share their orbits with other large objects.

Here are some more facts about Pluto, the most famous dwarf planet.

- Eek and Ack's giant magnifying glass must have been very powerful to melt Pluto's icy surface. Its average temperature is minus 230 degrees Celsius.

- One Pluto day equals six Earth days. One Pluto year equals 249 Earth years!

- An 11-year-old girl gave Pluto its name. Venetia Burney from Great Britain suggested the name after the Roman god of the underworld.

- Pluto is smaller than the Earth's moon.

- It takes five hours for sunlight to reach Pluto. It takes eight minutes for sunlight to reach Earth.

THE FUN DOESN'T STOP HERE!

DISCOVER MORE AT...

WWW.RAINTREEPUBLISHERS.CO.UK